Disney PRINCESS

Palace Pets

5-Minute Palace Pets Stories

Adapted by Sue Fliess

Illustrated by the Disney Storybook Art Team

DISNEY PRESS

Los Angeles • New York

Printed in the United States of America

First Edition, March 2015

1 3 5 7 9 10 8 6 4 2

Library of Congress Control Number: 2014940979

ISBN 978-1-4847-0463-9

G942-9090-6-15044

Visit www.disneybooks.com

Contents

A Prancing Puppy for Cinderella
&
The Garden Party

A Prancing Puppy for Cinderella

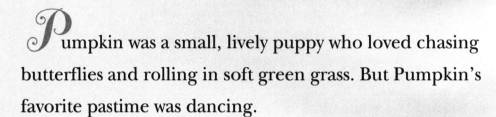

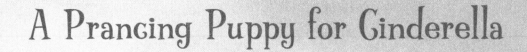

Pumpkin was a small, lively puppy who loved chasing butterflies and rolling in soft green grass. But Pumpkin's favorite pastime was dancing.

Pumpkin could whirl and twirl, sway and swirl, dip and dance the day away. It was her great wish to attend a royal ball, where she could waltz and sashay to the melodies of a master orchestra.

One day, the Prince arrived to pick out a puppy for Cinderella as an anniversary present. But he wasn't looking for just any puppy. No, the Prince was looking for a puppy as sweet and as special as Cinderella.

Pumpkin knew that this was her chance to make her dream come true!

Without wasting a minute, Pumpkin stood up on her hind legs and began to dance for the Prince. She hopped here, and she pranced there, and she twirled just about everywhere.

The Prince knew he had found the perfect anniversary gift for Cinderella! The princess would love a puppy with such pizzazz, and he was happy to give the little white pup a good home.

The Prince took Pumpkin back to the palace. He gave her a sparkly collar and a tiara. Then he gently placed her in a basket with a velvety-soft pillow out on the balcony. The Prince thought Pumpkin would make a perfect surprise for the princess at the anniversary ball later that night.

Pumpkin could hardly wait! She was finally going to attend a royal ball.

Pumpkin stretched as everyone bustled and bothered around her getting ready for the ball.

Musicians warmed up their instruments, cooks prepared a delicious feast, and servants busily hung the last of the decorations.

Before long, it was time for the ball to begin!

Meanwhile, Cinderella was thinking about how happy she was and how much she had to be thankful for.

Exactly one year earlier, Cinderella's fairy godmother and animal friends had helped make her dreams come true. The princess couldn't wait to celebrate her anniversary with the Prince at the ball that evening.

Soon the music swelled to a start and filled the grand
ballroom. Cinderella was ready to dance!

When at last the Prince and princess were alone on the
dance floor, the Prince told Cinderella how much he loved her.
Then he asked her for a special dance beneath the stars. He was
ready to surprise her with the sweet prancing puppy.

Cinderella and the Prince stepped out onto the balcony, and all was nearly perfect. The stars were shining, the moon was bright, and the music drifted through the night sky, but Pumpkin was nowhere to be seen!

The Prince wondered where the pup had run off to.

Thankfully, the surprise had not been spoiled!

Pumpkin had simply been so eager to enjoy the ball that she hadn't been able to sit still one second longer.

The Prince and princess soon spotted the missing pup on the other side of the balcony, dipping and dancing, hopping and prancing along to the music.

Cinderella had always wanted a puppy, and she was touched by the Prince's thoughtful anniversary gift. However, the princess was even more surprised by how talented her new pup was!

She admired Pumpkin's graceful twirls, and quickly joined in on the fun.

When the final song came to a close, Cinderella lifted Pumpkin and snuggled the pup into her arms.

Pumpkin had danced at a royal ball, and her dream had become a reality. But Pumpkin realized that an even greater wish had come true that night, for she now had a home with Cinderella and the Prince.

Cinderella and Pumpkin have been inseparable ever since. The princess delights in having a prancing puppy of her very own, and Pumpkin is so happy to be part of a loving family.

The two new friends dance together every day and enjoy one another's company in time with the music.

The Garden Party

It was a warm and wonderful day in Cinderella's garden. The birds chirped in the trees, the bees buzzed among the flowers, and the princess's sweet puppy was practicing her pirouettes.

Pumpkin was happy to be outside, sashaying in the sunshine, but she was soon distracted from her dance when she happened upon a plaything.

Pumpkin inspected the toy with care. She sniffed it, unsure what it could be, but when she got close, the plaything scooted away from her. She sneaked up on it again, and it flailed once more! Was it a snake?

The puppy followed the long blue something as it streaked through the garden, until . . .

. . . she was nose to nose with a mouse!

But this wasn't just any mouse. It was Cinderella's friend Gus. And the plaything was a long paper streamer!

Gus was startled by the puppy at first, but when he realized it was his old pal Pumpkin, he was delighted!

With a skip and a scurry, Gus took off running through the grass, trailing the paper streamer behind him for Pumpkin to chase.

The two friends bounded through begonias, dashed through daisies, and ran through roses. They dipped under dahlias, leaped over lilies, and pranced through peonies. The garden was the perfect playground!

Pumpkin and Gus soon tumbled into a clearing.

There, the puppy quickly learned that there was going to be a garden party that evening. Gus's fellow mouse, Jaq, was in charge of decorations, and Bibbidy, Cinderella's pony, was lending a helping hoof.

"I love parties!" Pumpkin exclaimed. "Can I help?"

Jaq wasn't sure how much help Pumpkin would be.

"All right," he finally agreed. "But everything needs to be perfect."

Poor Jaq was right: Pumpkin was not much help at all. In fact, she actually caused quite a bit of trouble!

The puppy tried to help trim the trees with long, paper streamers, but she found it was much more fun to twirl in them instead.

As Pumpkin twirled, Gus, Jaq, and Bibbidy decorated the garden with care.

When it was time to hang the lights, Pumpkin
was far too tangled up to help.

"Look at me! I'm just like a tree!" Pumpkin called
as her friends delicately hung the twinkling lights.

Jaq thought that Pumpkin could at least help them polish the dance floor. Her four paws were always moving, so they might as well be polishing.

The little puppy had another idea, though.

"Why polish when you can slide?" Pumpkin shouted.

But the real trouble started when Jaq asked Pumpkin to help him set the table. The little puppy just couldn't focus on forks and spoons when there were big, beautiful cupcakes nearby.

Pumpkin loved cupcakes! She decided it would be more helpful of her to sample one of them, to make sure they were tasty. Gus decided he would sample one, as well.

Sure enough, sampling turned into devouring, and soon Pumpkin and Gus had eaten every last cupcake.

"Those were for the party!" Jaq cried. "You are no help at all, Pumpkin!"

The little puppy felt bad that she had eaten the cupcakes. As she looked across the garden, she saw the streamers and lights hung with care and the perfectly polished dance floor. Her friends had worked so hard, and she had been nothing but trouble.

"I'm sorry," said Pumpkin.

Fortunately, there had been others helping prepare for the party. Someone had even brought a cake to replace the missing cupcakes.

There was no need for Jaq to worry. Everything was perfect, just as he had hoped.

That is, until the music started. The dance floor was empty!

Pumpkin knew just how she could help. She might not be good at hanging lights or streamers, polishing floors, or setting tables, but Pumpkin sure knew how to dance!

The little puppy rushed to the empty dance floor and immediately began to whirl and twirl. She pranced and danced and performed pretty pirouettes to the beat of the music. The party guests couldn't help joining Pumpkin . . .

. . . and neither could Cinderella!

Jaq was relieved. Pumpkin had saved the soiree after all.

The garden party was a huge success, and the four friends celebrated their hard work by dancing the night away under the stars with their favorite princess.

Berry

A Bashful Bunny for Snow White
&
The Big Rescue

A Bashful Bunny for Snow White

*B*erry was a little bunny who lived among a berry bramble in the forest. She loved hopping through the woods collecting big ripe blueberries. But this little bunny was terribly shy. Berry was so shy, in fact, that she would scurry away and hide whenever she encountered someone new.

One particularly bright summer day, the delicious smell of blueberries woke Berry from her slumber. With a stretch and a yawn, she was ready for breakfast!

The bushes were bursting with sweet blue fruit. There must have been thousands of berries within reach, and all of them were ripe for the picking! Hopping along, Berry plucked berry after berry, popping each one into her mouth.

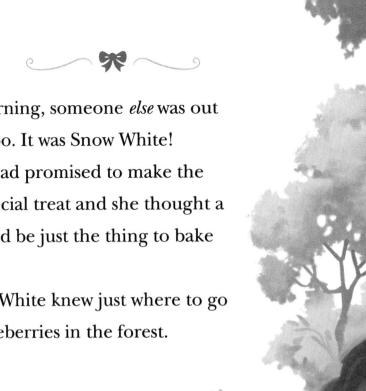

That same morning, someone *else* was out on a berry hunt, too. It was Snow White!

The princess had promised to make the Seven Dwarfs a special treat and she thought a blueberry pie would be just the thing to bake for them.

Luckily, Snow White knew just where to go to get the best blueberries in the forest.

Soon enough, Snow White found a pocket of bushes full of
ripe blueberries. She began picking the fruit carefully from the
branches, gently dropping each berry into her silver pail.

The pail was nearly full when she came upon a bush with the
biggest, juiciest blueberries of all.

Little did the princess know, a berry-loving bunny had already discovered that particular bush. Hiding among the branches, Berry wasn't about to let her beautiful blueberries go to someone else. So just as Snow White was about to pluck a berry, the bunny plucked it first.

Berry beat Snow White to every ripe blueberry in sight, one after the other.

Snow White was puzzled. Who could be snatching up the berries right before her eyes?

The princess tiptoed around the bush to take a look. She caught sight of a soft, fluffy tail, as white as snow, poking out from the thick green leaves.

Snow White knew that, whatever it was, there was something at the end of that tail that loved blueberries.

So she found the plumpest berry she had in her pail and placed it in her palm. Snow White knelt down next to the bush, held out her palm, and waited.

Slowly, a sweet little bunny hopped out.

When Berry saw the princess holding that big ripe berry, she no longer felt shy. Instead, she jumped onto Snow White's lap to eat the berry out of her hand.

Snow White was so taken by the fluffy little bunny that she let Berry eat berries out of her silver pail all afternoon.

Soon Snow White and the Prince had to leave the forest. The princess said good-bye to Berry and started walking down the path toward the palace, her pail of picked blueberries swinging at her side. But the little bunny just couldn't let that big bucket of berries disappear. She had to have those berries!

Without letting them see her, Berry followed the Prince and Snow White all the way home.

When Snow White got back to the castle, she set down her bucket of berries in the kitchen and started to gather the ingredients she would need for a pie. Suddenly, the pail began rocking back and forth before tipping over completely! Berries spilled out everywhere.

Imagine Snow White's surprise when she saw Berry the bunny tumble out of the pail, as well!

Thankfully, the bunny was nearly full of berries, so there were plenty left over for a pie for the Seven Dwarfs.

Now Berry lives with Snow White and the Prince in their castle. The bunny is so happy to have a new family of her own, and Snow White couldn't love her shy little friend more.

Every morning, Berry bounds out of bed to have breakfast with her princess. And while Snow White may have introduced Berry to new treats, blueberries are still the little bunny's favorite.

The Big Rescue

One afternoon, Berry was bounding through the forest. As she passed blueberry bush after blueberry bush, she plucked every berry in sight. The little bunny loved the taste of blueberries, but after eating so many of them that morning, she was thirsty. Berry decided to fetch a drink of water at the well.

As Berry hopped along, she remembered that wells weren't just for water—they were also for wishing. The little bunny knew that once upon a time, Snow White had made a wish at a well. The princess had wished that her prince would find her—and her wish came true!

Berry decided that when she got to the well, she would wish for a bucket of nice cold water to drink.

When Berry reached the well, she was excited to see that her wish was about to come true! There was a big wooden bucket sitting on the ledge of the well. Seeing the bucket made Berry even thirstier, so she hopped up onto the ledge of the well to get a closer look.

But just as Berry was about to peer into the bucket, the shy little bunny heard footsteps coming from the woods. The noise grew louder and louder as the footsteps trampled over twigs and leaves.

Crunch, crunch, crunch!

Berry was so startled by the strange sounds that she immediately hopped inside the bucket to hide.

She was much too shy to wait and see whom the footsteps belonged to.

After all, what if it was a monster, or some scary beast that liked to eat bunnies?

Unfortunately, Berry jumped inside the bucket so quickly that she accidentally knocked it from the ledge of the well.

The bucket was now dangling dangerously over the water, swinging back and forth—with Berry inside!

No problem, thought Berry. *I'll just hop right out!*

But whenever she tried to move, the bucket would tip and swing this way and that. Berry wasn't sure what to do.

The little bunny thought, pondered, and puzzled. How could she get out of the bucket?

Then Berry realized just how high she actually was. . . .

Fortunately, the mysterious footsteps belonged to Snow White's pony, Sweetie. The pony had been on a walk through the woods in search of her own delicious snack. In fact, Sweetie had picked up the scent of pie in the air, and she was hot on its trail. That is, until she was distracted by another trail—a trail of blueberries!

Sweetie followed the tasty trail. The berries led her to the well, where she noticed a peculiar sight . . . two bunny ears poking out of a bucket!

Blueberries and bunny ears can only mean one thing, thought Sweetie.

"Berry?" the pony asked. "Are you in there?"

"Yes!" said Berry. "I was thirsty, but now I'm thirsty and *stuck.* Can you please help me?"

"Of course!" Sweetie replied. "But how?"

Sweetie ambled around the well to investigate. It was pretty large, and the wall was rather high. She wasn't nearly as good of a hopper as Berry was, and her hooves could be clumsy sometimes. The last thing she wanted was to knock Berry out of the bucket by accident.

Finally, Sweetie formed a plan.

First she carefully placed her two front hooves on the ledge
of the well to steady herself. Then she stretched out her neck,
delicately used her teeth to grab on to the rope that was holding
the bucket, and, with a gentle tug, pulled Berry back to safety.

"Thank you!" said Berry as she gave Sweetie a hug.

The bunny was happy to be back on solid ground and very thankful that her good friend had appeared just in time to rescue her from the well.

"Come along," Sweetie said. "I think Snow White has baked a pie. I was following the scent before I found you. Can you smell it?"

Together the two friends hurried toward the castle. Berry had to hop extra fast to keep up with Sweetie. But when they finally reached the kitchen door, there wasn't a pie in sight!

"I thought for sure Snow White was baking!" said Sweetie.

"And I do smell something sweet," said Berry.

Berry and Sweetie were about to walk back to the forest when Snow White appeared at the door. "There are my two favorite pets!" the princess said. "I thought you might come by for a visit, so my friends and I made a treat for you!"

Then the princess came out of the kitchen holding a
freshly baked blueberry pie. Happy followed right behind
her with a second perfect pie.

Berry and Sweetie started to prance with glee. Each pet
was going to have a pie of her very own!

The two friends spent the rest of the afternoon out in the courtyard enjoying their pies and the warm sunshine.

Just as they finished eating, Dopey wandered by with a bucket filled with water.

Thank goodness! thought Berry. *I'm even thirstier than before!*

Bayou

A Perfect Pony for Tiana
&
The Missing Musician

A Perfect Pony for Tiana

$\mathcal{B}$ayou lived in the sleepy little country of Maldonia. It was a beautiful and peaceful land full of flowers, tall trees, and mountains. Bayou's days were spent grazing in quiet meadows, running through green pastures, and taking long naps in the palace garden.

But now Bayou was moving to a big city. She didn't know what a big city would be like. She wondered if she would still have meadows to run through, or a garden to take naps in. But what worried Bayou most of all was that she would miss her quiet life in Maldonia.

Bayou boarded a large ship with Prince Naveen's parents and they set sail for America. It was a very long voyage from Maldonia to the big city. They sailed across miles and miles of ocean, and the trip took many days. Bayou was beginning to think they'd *never* arrive.

Finally, the ship pulled into a harbor. Bayou looked up and saw that they had arrived at the Port of New Orleans—the city she would soon call home. When Bayou and Prince Naveen's parents stepped off the gangway, there was a lovely lady waiting for them. It was Princess Tiana!

Bayou was shy at first, but she was relieved to see that the princess was happy to meet her.

And Tiana had a welcome gift for Bayou. . . .

It was a costume!

Bayou had arrived on Fat Tuesday, just in time for the big Mardi Gras parade—a New Orleans tradition. Bayou had never seen a parade before! And this parade was a celebration, where everyone ate and danced to music and wore colorful masks and costumes.

But this was all new to Bayou. She had never worn a costume before and wasn't sure she'd like it. Suddenly, she missed her quiet home and wanted to go back.

Tiana could tell that Bayou was feeling uncertain. Luckily, the princess had just the thing to make Bayou smile.

Tiana welcomed the little pony to New Orleans with a slice of apple pie she had baked herself.

If there is one cure for homesickness, it's sharing a slice of pie with a new friend.

The piece of pie perked Bayou right up! And when the
pony heard the parade music begin, she couldn't help but twirl
and trot. The more she pranced, the better she felt. And as she
danced, she admired her costume, twinkling in the starlight.
Bayou decided that costumes weren't so bad after all.

The Mardi Gras parade was an amazing sight to see. The streets of New Orleans were decorated with twinkling lights, vibrant banners, and strands upon strands of brightly colored beads.

Bayou and Tiana watched as floats big and small went by. They loved seeing everyone in creative costumes. But Tiana still had one more surprise for Bayou.

Tiana led Bayou onto a float—and the two became part of the parade! To Bayou, being in the parade was even better than watching it!

As the crowd around the float clapped and cheered for the little pony, Bayou suddenly became very excited for her new life with Tiana in the big city.

The next day, Tiana introduced Bayou to her best friend, Charlotte LaBouff. Bayou would live in the stables at the LaBouffs' estate. There was even a large green pasture for Bayou to enjoy, and a garden perfect for afternoon naps.

Then Tiana took Bayou to her world-class restaurant in downtown New Orleans. Having her own restaurant was Tiana's dream come true—just as having a friend like Tiana was Bayou's.

Nowadays, Tiana and Bayou spend their time together exploring the big city. New Orleans is loud and lively and very different from Bayou's quiet palace in Maldonia, but the little pony has learned to love her jazzy new home—and she could never dream of leaving Tiana's side.

The Missing Musician

The streets of New Orleans were buzzing with excitement. Prince Naveen's jazz band was going to perform that very evening at Princess Tiana's restaurant!

Bayou couldn't wait for the concert. The little pony had a special spring in her step as she walked down the street with Tiana in the cool night air.

Tiana's kitten, Lily, waited at the front steps of the restaurant to greet the princess and Bayou. Tiana gave Lily a quick pet, and thanked Bayou for the escort, before she ducked inside to help prepare for the evening's festivities.

Both pets could tell that Tiana was a bit nervous. There was going to be a full house at the restaurant that night for the concert. Everything had to be perfect!

Bayou was excited to hear Prince Naveen and his star trumpet player, Louis, perform that evening. She was ready to prance and dance to the music. But as soon as Tiana was out of sight, Lily pulled Bayou aside and whispered, "Louis is late!"

"But the band can't play without Louis!" Bayou replied. "What should we do?"

Lily and Bayou looked through the window of the restaurant and saw all of the guests eagerly waiting for the concert to begin.

The animals knew that everyone would be disappointed if Louis didn't show up. And the last thing Tiana needed was a restaurant full of unhappy customers.

Lily and Bayou had to do something to save the show, and they had to do it quickly!

"The show must go on!" said Lily. "Let's find Louis!"

Then she led the way down the cobblestone streets of New Orleans, with her best pony pal right on her tail.

As they hurried toward the bayou where Louis lived, a few fireflies joined the pets to light their way. Bayou and Lily were thankful for the fireflies as their surroundings grew darker the farther they ran from the city lights.

As they walked down the path, Lily and Bayou could hear crickets chirping throughout the marsh, frogs croaking down by the water, and owls hooting from up in the trees. It was as though there was a whole orchestra hiding just out of sight!

Lily's tail rustled like the brush of a jazz drum against the bushes: *swish, swish, swishity-swish.*

Meanwhile, Bayou's hooves beat on the cobblestones, low and full, like a stand-up bass: *bum, bum, bum-diddy-bum.*

Bayou liked the way her hooves sounded on the stones and wondered what it would be like to be in a real band. With Lily's tail and Bayou's hooves, maybe they could make their own music!

Soon the fireflies that had led Lily and Bayou through the marsh joined hundreds of their twinkling friends. The fireflies surrounded a little old house in a sparkly glow.

It was Louis's home!

The alligator's windows were open, and Lily and Bayou could hear Louis snoring inside. They needed to wake him up right away, but how?

Louis had fallen asleep because he had been practicing for
the big performance all day.

Suddenly, something stirred him from his slumber. . . .

Bum, bum, bum-diddy-bum. Swish, swish, swish.

Bum, bum, bum-diddy-bum. Swish, swish, swish.

Lily and Bayou's jazzy beats were all Louis needed to jump up out of bed.

"The concert!" Louis cried.

The alligator grabbed his trumpet, and the three friends made their way back through the marsh, making music together as they hurried along.

Lily, Bayou, and Louis reached the restaurant just in time, and the trumpet star didn't waste another minute. He hopped on stage with Prince Naveen and the band began to play.

The dinner guests cheered! The band performed song after song, deep into the night, but the audience still wanted more.

Lily and Bayou enjoyed the concert, too. They danced and pranced, and even added their own melodies from time to time.

When the concert finally ended, there was not one unhappy customer in sight. The evening had been perfect!

When it was time to go home, Princess Tiana came outside and thanked Bayou and Lily. She knew it must have been her two favorite pets who had saved the show.

Lily and Bayou may make great music together, but they make an even better team.

Treasure

A Curious Kitten for Ariel
&
The Ocean Voyage

A Curious Kitten for Ariel

Treasure was not like other kittens. Most cats are afraid of water, but the beach was Treasure's favorite place to play. She would chase crabs, splash in the waves, and walk along the shore collecting sparkly trinkets, shiny seashells, and beautiful gifts from the sea.

But even though she loved being a beach kitten, whenever Treasure looked out over the wide ocean, she wanted to explore. She dreamed of sailing the seven seas!

One morning, Treasure saw a magnificent vessel docked
nearby. She had never been on a real ship before and wanted to
get a closer look. This was her chance for a great adventure!

Treasure ran across the sand and hopped over rocks to get to
the dock. When she reached the gangway, she looked around to
see if anyone was watching. Then she quickly tiptoed on board.

As Treasure started to nose around the deck, the ship began pulling away from port! She had never been away from her beach before—she was very excited!

As the ship sailed off, Treasure wondered where it would take her. Would she go to the desert? To the mountains? To a big bustling city?

Wherever the ship was headed, Treasure was sure she would find new friends and fun trinkets along the way.

Treasure wasn't sure how long the journey would be, so she found a hiding place to take a nap.

The gentle sway of the ship was sure to lull her to sleep soon enough. But just as she got cozy, Treasure noticed the ship's crew had gathered all around her!

The little kitten tried to run away, but one of the crewmen picked her up before she could escape.

Treasure was scared; she hadn't meant to cause trouble. What would the crew do with a stowaway kitten? Would they make her scrub the deck? Would the captain force her to walk the plank?

Instead, the crew handed Treasure to a handsome young man—it was Prince Eric! Treasure hadn't known at the time, but she had snuck onto the prince's royal ship. As Prince Eric held the curious little kitten with her soft red fur, he couldn't help but think of someone else whom he loved very much.

That special someone was Princess Ariel. And the princess would be boarding the royal ship that very day. Prince Eric announced that he would adopt Treasure for Ariel. The little red kitten was so excited to finally have a home of her own!

All hands and paws were on deck to prepare for Ariel's arrival. Treasure helped polish the helm until it shined. She pulled long ropes to raise the royal flag. And she collected sparkly trinkets she found on board to decorate every nook and cranny of the ship.

Then Treasure pranced along the bow with anticipation. The wind ruffled her fur and the salty spray from the waves tickled her nose. She hoped Ariel would like her as much as Prince Eric did.

As the prince led Princess Ariel on board, a sea breeze blew a string of seashells next to Treasure. When the kitten leaped up to paw at the shells, the sound caught Ariel's attention. She turned to see Treasure, a kitten with red fur the same color as her own red hair.

Ariel picked up the kitten and cuddled her close. Treasure smelled of the sea, which reminded Ariel of her friends beneath the waves. This made Ariel very happy. Treasure was happy, too. She purred and felt warm and safe in the princess's arms.

As the ship sailed around the harbor, a party commenced to celebrate Ariel—and her new kitten. There was a great feast on board with the finest food anyone could ask for, and lively music for everyone to enjoy.

When the ship returned to port, Treasure followed Ariel and Eric up the sandy path to their castle, which had a beautiful view of the ocean.

Ariel gave Treasure her very own bed and more trinkets to play with than the kitten could ever have imagined.

Ariel then placed a jeweled collar around Treasure's neck and a special tiara between her soft ears. But the most special gift that Ariel gave Treasure that day was a new home. Treasure was so happy to live with her princess in the royal palace.

Now Ariel takes Treasure down to the beach every day to explore. They swim and jump through the waves together. They run after crabs, chase seagulls, and walk along the shore, collecting trinkets and treasures and dreaming of future adventures on the high seas.

Treasure is still a little beach kitten, but now she is a beach kitten with a best friend.

The Ocean Voyage

One afternoon, Treasure and her friends were playing together in the sand.

As Treasure walked along the shore looking for trinkets to add to her collection, she saw something big on the beach, far off in the distance. The kitten quickly ran to get a closer look, with her friends trailing behind her.

To Treasure's delight, the mysterious something was a wooden rowboat! For a water-loving kitten, this was the best treasure of all.

If only it wasn't stuck in the sand, she thought, *I could sail the high seas all afternoon!*

Treasure jumped in the boat anyway and announced, "All aboard!"

However, Treasure's friends were not nearly as eager to explore the open ocean as she was. As Ariel's seagull friend Scuttle eyed the boat warily, Max, Prince Eric's sheepdog, inspected the boat with a sniff. Meanwhile, Sebastian the crab clutched the bow, frozen with fear.

But as long as the boat was beached safely on the sand, Treasure's friends decided there was no harm in *pretending* to voyage across the seven seas.

The friends imagined they were the captain and crew of a big ship. Treasure called out commands to her sailors, and kept a lookout for any danger off in the distance.

She made her crew work hard, scrubbing the deck, pulling on ropes, and keeping the boat in tip-top shape.

The friends were having a great time when, out of the blue,
a gigantic wave rolled onto the beach and pulled them right
off the sand—and into the open water! Now Treasure and her
friends were actually afloat at sea!

Treasure didn't know where the current was taking them, but she was too excited to give it a second thought.

She peeked her head over the edge of the boat and found her reflection staring back at her in the water below. A pod of friendly dolphins playfully swam nearby, quickly jumping in and out of the waves as though they were enjoying a game of tag.

Meanwhile, Sebastian was worried that they were floating too far from home. And Max started to whimper at the sight of gray storm clouds rolling in.

Max was right to worry. The sky grew darker and stormier, and thunder rumbled off in the distance. Soon heavy raindrops began to fall from the clouds, one by one.

But Captain Treasure knew just what to do.

"Batten down the hatches!" she shouted.

The crew may have been prepared for a little rain, but to Treasure's surprise, it began to pour!

The friends tried to paddle back toward land, but the stormy weather turned the boat this way and that, rocking them up and down. All they could do was hold on.

Thankfully, almost as suddenly as the storm rolled in, it rolled back out again. The rain stopped, the waves died down, and the dark clouds melted away into a bright blue sky. The captain and crew hugged one another and cheered.

And when the friends looked up, they were treated to a beautiful rainbow.

Soon a gentle wave carried their boat back to the beach, and they were safe on shore once again.

Treasure had learned her lesson about the ocean. It might be beautiful, but it could also be dangerous. She decided right then and there that she would only embark on sea voyages when she was with Prince Eric and his trusty crew of sailors.

Prince Eric and Princess Ariel were waiting for Max and
Treasure back at the beach. Max bounded over to Prince Eric
and gave him a big lick on his chin. Treasure ran to Ariel and
cuddled up against the princess, purring.

"Now what have you two been up to?" Ariel wondered as she
scratched the little red kitten under the chin.

Max and Treasure looked at one another with a secret smile, for Eric and Ariel would never know about their exciting afternoon at sea.

As they walked back to the castle, the two friends agreed they had had enough adventure for one day. But it was certainly an adventure Treasure would never forget.

A Playful Panda for Mulan
&
The Great Market Chase

A Playful Panda for Mulan

One evening, a happy little panda bear named Blossom was wandering through a forest of bamboo. She was looking for a special snack.

It was mid-autumn, and the days were getting shorter. As the sky darkened, the little panda's tummy gave a rumble. She looked all around her for something to eat besides bamboo. Where could she find a tasty treat?

Ever cheerful, Blossom didn't give up hope. By the light of the moon, the panda walked toward a little town nearby.

It was very quiet, but as she neared the village, she could hear people laughing and talking. She heard music playing, too. But best of all, wonderful smells wafted about her.

Food! Blossom thought as she followed her nose to an ornate wooden gate.

The gate was much too tall for a little panda to climb over. Blossom decided that she would have to go under it to get to the other side.

So with a squirm and a squeeze, the panda managed to crawl under the gate. And when Blossom looked up from the ground, she was amazed by what she saw.

The village was decorated for the big Moon Festival! Colorful
lanterns lit up the night sky, and a giant dragon shimmied and
shook through the crowded street. Everyone was celebrating and
dancing to the music.

Best of all, Blossom saw that there were banquet tables
covered with food for as far as the eye could see. She couldn't
believe her good fortune!

Blossom's tummy rumbled and grumbled with hunger as she
reached for a snack.

But before Blossom could begin her feast, someone suddenly shouted, "A bear!"

A bear! thought a frightened Blossom. *Where?*

She couldn't see a bear anywhere, but she didn't want to stick around until one appeared. Instead, she dashed into the crowd to hide.

Blossom ran around tables, darted between guests'
feet, and finally ducked beneath the parading dragon.
Surely I'll be safe here! she thought.

Once under the dragon, the little panda couldn't help shimmying and shaking right along with the parade!

The dragon danced to the right, so Blossom danced to the right. And when the dragon danced to the left, Blossom danced to the left, too.

She was having such a good time that she forgot all about the bear everyone was running from.

That is, until she was spotted. . . .

They must not want me dancing along with the dragon, Blossom thought as the guests scattered around her.

However, to the little panda's delight, she noticed that she was right in front of a giant table full of food. All of that dancing had made her even hungrier than before, and she was ready to eat!

Just as Blossom was about to start her feast, a beautiful girl walked up to the banquet table.

It was Mulan!

Mulan didn't seem worried about a bear. In fact, she seemed just as happy as Blossom to have a whole table of food to herself.

Mulan loved the Moon Festival. Every year, she looked forward to the special night filled with music, dancing, lanterns, dragons, and fun.

But Mulan's favorite part of the festival was eating moon cakes, and there was a mountain of them right in front of her.

The princess couldn't wait to eat some of the special cakes, but just as Mulan reached for one, the tower of cakes collapsed!

The soft, sweet treats tumbled across the table and down to the ground.

It was a very sad sight.

Mulan was puzzled.

"Why did all of the cakes fall?" she asked herself as she gathered the scattered cakes from the table.

Mulan found her answer when she reached down to clean up the moon cakes that had fallen to the ground.

There, sitting in a pile of moon cakes, was the cutest little panda she had ever seen. Blossom had pulled a cake from the bottom of the pile, which had caused the tower of sweets to collapse.

"It looks like someone *else* loves moon cakes as much as I do," Mulan said with a chuckle.

"It's okay, little one," said Mulan. "I'm not scared of panda bears."

The princess lifted Blossom into the night sky. The full moon glowed against the panda's periwinkle fur.

"I think we are going to be very good friends," Mulan told Blossom.

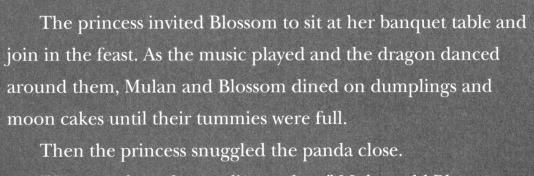

The princess invited Blossom to sit at her banquet table and
join in the feast. As the music played and the dragon danced
around them, Mulan and Blossom dined on dumplings and
moon cakes until their tummies were full.

Then the princess snuggled the panda close.

"You can always be my dinner date," Mulan told Blossom.

In keeping with tradition, Mulan lit a lantern at the end
of the festival. Then she made a wish and released it into the
night sky.

    As the lantern floated away, the princess knew her wish had
already come true, for she now had a sweet little panda bear of
her very own.

And Blossom's wish came true, too. She finally had a place to call home.

These days, Blossom and Mulan spend time together exploring bamboo forests and enjoying fine meals.

Now Blossom is never far from a snack. But more importantly, she is never far from her new friend.

The Great Market Chase

It was market day, Mulan's favorite day of the week. She loved exploring the maze of outdoor stalls and finding the freshest fruits and vegetables.

That day, Mulan was gathering ingredients for a special meal.

"Blossom, be a good panda while I'm gone," the princess said. "You behave, too, Mushu. And both of you stay put until I return!"

Blossom loved market day almost as much as Mulan did. Just thinking about all the wonderful food made her tummy rumble.

Mushu's tummy rumbled, too.

The two looked at each other and smiled.

"Let's go!" they both shouted.

Blossom didn't see the harm in getting a quick snack.

Cri-Kee squeaked his concern. But Blossom and Mushu had made up their minds to go. So when the little panda and dragon squeezed through the open window, all Cri-Kee could do was hop after them and hope for the best.

The market was bustling. It was a beautiful day, so everyone
was outside enjoying the sunshine and the stalls were stacked
high with piles of bright fruits and vegetables.

The sweet and savory smells were almost too much for the
three friends to bear. Blossom, Mushu, and Cri-Kee couldn't wait
to find a yummy snack.

Blossom and Mushu came to a screeching halt in front of a colorful fruit stand. Everything looked so delicious it was hard to choose!

Apple or pear? thought the panda bear.

Blossom eventually decided on a bright yellow pomelo, while Mushu picked up a dragon fruit. Both devoured their fruit in a flash.

Then Blossom and Mushu visited a vegetable stand nearby! It was just as colorful as the fruit stand. Purple eggplant, blue potatoes, yellow squash, green beans, and . . . a cricket?

Cri-Kee hopped about collecting as many beans as he could carry.

Then the friends came across a large stack of lemons. The yellow fruit smelled refreshing. Blossom thought they must taste delicious, so she took a big lick of the juicy treat.

Looks are deceiving, Blossom decided as the sour tang made her wince.

When Blossom, Mushu, and Cri-Kee spotted a barrel of peppers, they dove right in.

"Delicious!" said Mushu as he took a bite and breathed fire.

"Yikes!" said Blossom, fanning her mouth and looking around for something to drink.

Blossom spotted a fountain, so she dashed toward it, with the cricket right behind her.

After those spicy peppers, the water was crisp and refreshing.

The friends took a long drink, then splashed water at one another to cool off.

Mushu was about to make the biggest splash of all when he spotted Mulan. She was headed right for them!

"Blossom! Cri-Kee! Quick! Hide!" he half whispered, half shrieked. "Mulan is coming!"

Blossom had to think fast on her paws—and hide in plain sight!

Blossom's hiding place worked! Mulan hadn't spotted them.
Mushu and Cri-Kee were thankful to have such a clever friend.

Blossom knew that they needed to get back home soon, before
Mulan, but she couldn't leave the market without a sweet treat.

Just then, Blossom saw the stand she had been looking for all along. There were piles of cakes, mountains of treats, and all kinds of sweets.

Blossom dashed toward the cake stand as fast as her little paws would take her. Mushu and Cri-Kee could hardly keep up!

Blossom weaved through the crowd with ease, but when
she arrived at the cake stand, there were only crumbs left.
Someone had taken the very last cake!
The little panda was heartbroken.

When Mushu and Cri-Kee finally caught up to Blossom, they could see how disappointed she was.

"It's all right," said Mushu, putting his arm around her. "We'll get you a cake next week."

But Cri-Kee was too busy jumping up and down to comfort Blossom. He was trying to tell them something.

Blossom finally understood Cri-Kee's plea. "We need to get home before Mulan!"

The three friends ran, hopped, and dashed as fast as they could up the hill toward home. The journey back from the market seemed to take much longer than it had on their way there earlier in the day.

When they finally arrived, they were out of breath, but relieved to see no sign of Mulan.

"I think we made it," said Mushu.

But as they climbed back through the window, they smelled something wonderful wafting from the kitchen, and that could mean only one thing.

"Uh-oh," Blossom whispered. "Mulan beat us here."

The three friends were nervous. They were in real trouble now. . . .

"Time for dinner!" Mulan called from the dining room.

To their surprise, the table was filled with delicious dishes and set for four.

Mulan was serving all the fruits and vegetables she had bought at the market. But Blossom saw the most important dish in the center of the table: the very last sweet cake.

After a long day of markets and mischief, and with her belly full, Blossom was ready for bed.

As the panda settled into sleep that night, she knew she would dream of only one thing: the next market day!

Teacup

A Performing Puppy for Belle
&
The Shortcut

A Performing Puppy for Belle

Teacup was a peppy little puppy with lots of talent. She could stand on her hind legs, and walk on her front paws, but her signature move was balancing a teacup on her head. It's how she got her name! And she loved nothing more than performing for everyone in the village square.

Every day, Teacup put on a show for the villagers, hoping someone would notice her and make her a star.

Some days, Teacup found it easy to shine. People would stop what they were doing to watch the little puppy perform. Then they would applaud and reward her with lots of yummy treats!

On other days, however, Teacup found it hard to shine.

When a storm rolled in, the villagers stayed inside their warm homes and shops. No one ventured outside or seemed to be in the mood to watch Teacup perform.

On those days, Teacup wished that she, too, had a home to go to when the weather got dreary.

But Teacup knew that the show must go on. So on the next bright morning, the little puppy would be back at her spot in the village square, performing her signature move.

One sunny day, the puppy had just balanced the teacup on her head when she saw a beautiful girl walk by. Teacup took a closer look and realized it wasn't just any girl—it was Belle! Teacup had seen the princess from afar before, but today Belle stopped to watch the puppy perform. Teacup knew this was her chance to show Belle that she could be a star.

But as Teacup teetered and tottered to keep the teacup
balanced on her head, a beam of sunlight reflected off one of
Belle's golden earrings, momentarily blinding the peppy little pup!

That moment was just long enough for Teacup to lose her
balance. The teacup atop her head wiggled, then wobbled,
then toppled to the ground! The delicate little teacup hit the
cobblestones and shattered.

Poor Teacup!

What was the pup to do without her cup? She didn't know what else to perform now that her best trick was ruined.

The villagers began walking away one by one. Teacup tried to think of something else to make them stay, but it was no use.

The little puppy sat staring at the broken pieces at her feet.

To Teacup's surprise, when she looked up from the cup, Belle was still there. The princess had stayed!

Belle knew it was her fault that the teacup was broken, and she wanted to make things right. She knelt down and picked up the broken pieces.

"I'll help you get this teacup fixed in no time," said Belle. "And you're too great a star to stay out on the street. You should come live with me in the castle!"

Teacup knew the princess was kind, so she leaped into her arms, and Belle carried her all the way home.

Later that evening, the puppy was presented with her special
teacup, perfectly repaired. And not only had Belle fixed the cup,
she had prepared lots of delicious treats for Teacup, as well!

There were fruit plates and sandwiches, biscuits and cakes.
Belle even gave Teacup a beautiful tiara and a big bow for her tail
as a way to welcome the puppy to her new home.

Teacup had always dreamed of being noticed. Now she is Belle's little star, performing just for the princess.

She plays songs on the harp and balances all kinds of cups and saucers on her head.

But Teacup still makes time to perform in the village square.

The villagers always stop to watch Princess Belle's puppy, Teacup, put on a show.

Teacup and Belle go to the village square when the sun is shining, so that Teacup can shine, too. But when it rains, Teacup is happy to stay inside and enjoy the comfort of her new home.

The Shortcut

One bright morning, Teacup bounded toward town. She had a show to perform in the village square and she was already running a little late. So Teacup decided to take a shortcut through the forest.

As Teacup skipped through the woods, forest animals came out of their trees and burrows to say hello.

The bunnies, raccoons, squirrels, chipmunks, and birds were all eager to meet the famous performing pup. They hoped that Teacup would put on a special show for them.

Teacup could never turn down an audience. So the little puppy began to perform her signature trick, but this time she balanced a pinecone on her head. She even twirled around without letting it fall!

But soon the village clock chimed in the distance. It was nearly time for the puppy's performance in town.

Teacup knew if she didn't leave then, she would surely miss her own show. She didn't want to disappoint the villagers— or Belle!

The pup said a quick good-bye to her new friends and promised to come back soon, then she raced into the woods.

Teacup ran as fast as she could down the path. She leaped over bushes and ducked under branches with ease, and all the while she thought about her upcoming show.

The little puppy was so preoccupied, in fact, that she stopped paying attention to where she was running. Soon Teacup was lost. The forest around her was entirely unfamiliar.

Teacup sat in a small clearing, alone and upset.

The pup would surely miss her performance now. And what if she never found her way back to Belle?

Teacup didn't know what to do.

The pup was about to cry when she heard a rustle and a snort. Was it a lion? A bear? Teacup was scared. She dashed off to hide in the bushes.

The strange sounds grew closer and closer.

Poor Teacup! She was late, she was lost, and now she had a monster to worry about!

"Teacup?" called Petit, Belle's favorite pony.

"Oh, Petit!" said Teacup, popping out from behind the bushes. "You frightened me!"

"I'm sorry," said Petit. "Shouldn't you be at the village square?"

"I'm lost," cried Teacup, "and I'm late for my show! Can you help me?"

"Jump on," Petit replied. "I'll give you a ride to town."

Petit could run much faster than Teacup. And since the little pony knew the way through the woods, Teacup was sure they would get to the village in time.

Teacup was so relieved. And it was such great fun to ride on Petit's back! It even gave the puppy a brilliant idea for her upcoming show. . . .

When they reached town, Teacup stood on her hind legs on Petit's back. Together they made a grand entrance into the village square. The crowd cheered with delight!

That day, Teacup performed all of her tricks with Petit. They made a great team, and the villagers had never seen anything like it!

When someone shouted, "Bravo!" they knew it was Belle. She was Teacup and Petit's biggest fan. The pair took a deep bow as everyone applauded. After the show, Teacup, Petit, and Belle headed home, but not before making one special stop along the way.

Teacup introduced Belle and Petit to all of her new forest friends. They gathered around Teacup and she did a few more tricks for them, this time with Petit!

From that day on, Teacup and Petit always went through the forest together, and the little puppy never lost her way again.